Julia Gaile Quijano
Gia Janina Quijano
Jenevieve Gabrielle
Quijano
01 August 2018

TUCKER TIMES

THE CHASE

Genella Macintyre

Illustrated By
Morgan Spicer

BROWN BOOKS KIDS

Tucker Times
The Chase

Brown Books Kids
16250 Knoll Trail Drive, Suite 205
Dallas, Texas 75248
www.BrownBooksKids.com
(972) 381-0009

New Era in Publishing™

ISBN 978-1-61254-871-5
LCCN 2015950803

Printed in the United States
10 9 8 7 6 5 4 3 2 1

For more information or to contact the author, please go to
www.PartnersInDiscovery.com

To Anna, Tucker's biological mom, and Marie, Anna's owner who made sure Tucker thrived. And to Amber, a kindred spirit in making dreams happen.

Tucker is a lively pup
who loves to run and play.

So taking Tucker for long walks
is needed every day.

Now sometimes,

along the way,

things suddenly

appear!

But just as Tucker runs to them,

his Mama says, "No, dear!"

"Chasing squirrels is not what we do,

'cause they have to share the world with you.

Chasing birds is not what we do.
It's a waste of time, 'cause they'll fly past you.

Chasing cats is not what we do,

'cause they might bat you black and blue.

Chasing dogs is not what we do,
unless they're your friends, and they're playing with you.

Chasing toys—now that's what we do!

Bring Mama the ball,

and she'll throw it for you.

Now it's time for you to rest,

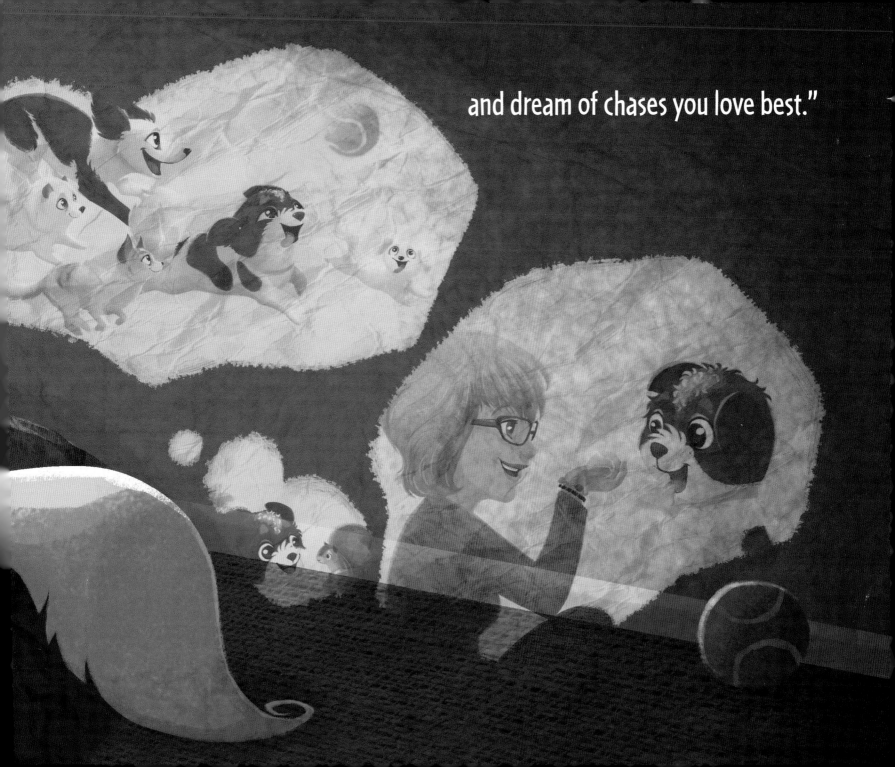

and dream of chases you love best."

ACKNOWLEDGMENTS

I would like to thank those people, complete strangers, who stopped and went, "Ahhhh, what a cute and special dog!"

Thank you, as well, to my husband Doug, who helped me raise Tucker to become the good boy he is today. Thanks to his godparents, Lynda and Jim, his Uncle Bob and Auntie Gloria for their special relationship with Tucker, and Linda K. for taking him for runs when Mama was away. And, of course, thanks to all the "Aunties" at Tucker's daycare, Woofs 'n Wags.

My sincerest appreciation to Morgan Spicer who illustrated this book and captured Tucker's spirit so well. Thanks, as well, to Keywest Photo Image by Design Inc. in Brandon, Manitoba, who took such great photos of Tucker. And finally, thank you to my publisher, Brown Books. My warm welcome from Sherry, head of the Brown Books Kids division, helped to begin a creative and nurturing relationship with the people who make up its staff. Caring and quality: this was exactly what I was looking for in a publishing company.

ABOUT THE AUTHOR

Genella Macintyre is a corporate trainer who lives in Brandon, Manitoba. She is the president of Partners in Discovery Ltd., a company designed to help organizations and individuals improve the quality of personal and professional living. She has a BA from Brandon University and received her MA in applied psychology from the University of Saskatchewan. Genella and her husband Doug are avid animal lovers, knowing the gifts that animals, whether they be with fur or with scales, can bring us. She is currently working on another book concerning stress management.

Spread joy where you can, give what you can, and take care of yourself and those around you: this is the philosophy that led Genella to write *Tucker Times: The Chase*, her first children's book.

ABOUT THE ILLUSTRATOR

Morgan Spicer is a children's book illustrator and the founder of Bark Point Studio. She has also designed album covers, children's pajamas, and children's board games, and she has worked as a background and character designer for PBS Sprout's *Sing It, Laurie!* She designs characters and concepts for animation while also creating custom animal art for her many Bark Point Studio fans. Morgan has created over 1,000 portraits, with a percentage of many of her commissions going to local and international animal rescue groups.